Abracadabra!

YEEPS!
Secret in the Statue!

D0376658

Anything can happen when you wave your magic wand!

Join the Abracadabra Club in all their Magical Mysteries.

#1: **POOF!** Rabbits Everywhere!

#2: **BOO!** Ghosts in the School!

#3: **PRESTO!** Magic Treasure!

#4: **YEEPS!** Secret in the Statue!

Abracadabra!

YEEPS!
Secret in the Statue!

By Peter Lerangis
Illustrated by Jim Talbot

A
LITTLE APPLE
PAPERBACK

SCHOLASTIC INC.

New York   Toronto   London   Auckland   Sydney
Mexico City   New Delhi   Hong Kong   Buenos Aires

This book is dedicated to the great teachers
at the New York City Lower Lab School.

No part of this work may be reproduced in whole or
in part, or stored in a retrieval system, or transmitted in
any form or by any means, electronic, mechanical,
photocopying, recording, or otherwise, without written
permission of the publisher. For information regarding
permission, write to Scholastic Inc., Attention:
Permissions Department,
557 Broadway, New York, NY 10012.

ISBN 0-439-22233-8

Copyright © 2002 by Peter Lerangis.
All rights reserved. Published by Scholastic Inc.
SCHOLASTIC, LITTLE APPLE, and associated logos are
trademarks and/or registered trademarks of Scholastic Inc.

12 11 10 9 8 7 6 5 4 3 2 1   2 3 4 5 6 7/0

Printed in the U.S.A.   40
First Scholastic printing, March 2002

Contents

Abracadabra!

YEEPS!
Secret in the Statue!

1

The Dreaded, Ancient, Golden Pig-lion-o-dile

"ATTENTION, ABRACADABRA CLUB!" yelled Jessica Frimmel. "LISTEN UP! I HAVE IMPORTANT NEWS TODAY!"

Jessica could do two things very, very well. Bossing People Around was one of them. She was loud. Indoors and out. She wanted things done Just Her Way and Just When She Wanted Them.

Doing magic tricks was the other.

As Main Brain of the Rebus Elementary School Abracadabra Club, she could do both. She was in charge of all meetings. She knew every one of the club's magic tricks. She even knew what "A.B.R.A.C.A.D.A.B.R.A." stood for.

"THIS MEETING OF . . ." she took a deep breath and went on, ". . . THE *AMAZING BETTER-REBUS-AREA COMPANY OF AMATEUR DETECTIVES AND BAFFLING REAL-MAGIC ARTISTS . . .* WILL COME TO ORDER!"

On that Tuesday, no one was listening to Jessica at all. It was the great opening of the Vorpal magic treasure chest. The chest had been given to them by a magician named Mr. Vorpal, and it was full of amazing stuff.

Selena Cruz danced by in a long dress. She passed a red feather under Jessica's nose. As official Club Designer, Selena was in charge of the group's style. She drew all the signs. She made all the sets and costumes for their magic shows. She would have designed everyone's hair, but no one would let her. Hair was very important to Selena. She brushed hers about a million times a day. "Did you say *order*, daaarling Jessica?" she said with a silly accent. "I order a brand-new diamond ring!"

"Your wish is my command!" shouted Max Bleeker, waving a white marble wand that he'd found in the chest. Mr. Beamish, the teacher in charge, called Max the club Numa. No one really knew what a "Numa" was. It could have meant vice president or floor sweeper, or grasshopper or teapot. But Max was sure it meant "wizard," mostly because he believed he *was* a wizard. He even wore a cape and top hat to school every day. "Alakazam, alakazing — I will make you a brand-new ring!"

Max's wand nearly poked Quincy Norton in the glasses. But Quincy didn't notice. For one thing, his glasses were always dirty around the edges. Quincy sometimes forgot simple things — like tying his shoes and cleaning his glasses. For another thing, he was busy pulling something out of the chest. Something heavy and wrapped in yellow paper.

Jessica cleared her throat once again. *"AHEM. I SAID . . . I CALL THIS MEETING OF THE ABRACADABRA CLUB TO ORDER!"*

"No, that's *not* what you said," Quincy replied. "You said, and I quote, 'This meeting of the Amazing Better-Rebus-Area Company of Amateur Detectives and Baffling Real-Magic Artists will come to order!'"

"Same thing!" Jessica snapped.

"Not exactly," Quincy replied.

Very, very smart people could be very,

very annoying. And Quincy was very, very smart. He was the club Scribe, or secretary. He loved to write. He took notes about *everything*. His backpack was stuffed with notepads. One notepad was for the Abracadabra Files, where he recorded the club's magic tricks. Another was the Club Meeting Journal. But his two favorites were the Mystery Log and the Clues Book.

Officially, the Abracadabra Club was a "Magic and *Mystery*" Club. And as Quincy pulled back the yellow paper, he came face-to-face with the club's newest mystery.

It was the head of a small, black crocodile with a missing eye.

"Yeeps!" Quincy cried, leaping back. The thing slipped out of the paper and fell to the table with a thud.

Its skin looked soft and wrinkled, but it made a hard sound like metal. Its chest was

large and furry like a lion's, its lower body like a sitting pig. One eye was a deep hole, the other a big red jewel.

The thing landed on its back, and Jessica saw its face clearly. Its snout was twisted into a strange smile. Its eye seemed to glow.

Jessica's mouth went dry. "Is it . . . alive?"

"Oh, my," said Mr. Beamish, their teacher, tugging on his pointy little beard. "Oh, my, my, my."

"Stay away!" Max said. "I sense powerful magic."

"You always sense powerful magic," Selena replied. "It's just a dirty old statue."

Quincy brought a white cloth napkin to school every day. He pulled it from his pocket and began wiping off the statue. The black color began to change.

"It's — it's — solid GOLD!" Selena

exclaimed. She took out her brush and began brushing her hair about a hundred miles an hour.

The sight of gold did that to Selena.

Quincy gave the statue a shake. "There's something inside."

"Ah," said Mr. Beamish. "In ancient times, valuable treasures were always hidden in strange, mythical beasts."

"Let's ask Mr. Skupa for a hammer . . ." Jessica said.

"*You can't break it!*" Selena shouted. "It must be worth a mint!"

"A whole case of mints," Max added.

Jessica took the statue. It felt warm and smooth. A thin crack ran from top to bottom, and on one side were two tiny hinges. She turned the statue over in her hand, looking for a secret button or switch. She tried not to look at the angry red eye. It was only a jewel, but it scared her.

Then she saw something she didn't expect. It was a hole, where another eye was supposed to be. Around the hole's edges was a thin metal ring. "Look," she said. "It's some kind of clip!"

Quincy leaned in. "Spring-loaded, I'll bet. As you put the eye in, a spring draws back inside the statue. Then it snaps back to keep the eye in place."

"That's it!" Jessica said. "That's the secret way to get inside the statue! The eye snaps in, and the latch opens."

"Interesting idea," said Mr. Beamish.

Quincy pushed his glasses up on his nose. "I was about to think of it myself."

"So if we find the other eye, we can unlock the secret treasure?" Selena said.

"Perhaps." Mr. Beamish was digging around in the magic treasure chest. "The eye is not in here. It may have been lost years and years ago."

"Maybe the statue can help us!" Max said, touching his fingers to his forehead. "I, MAX THE MAGNIFICENT, SHALL MAKE CONTACT THROUGH THE SPIRIT WORM . . ."

"Spirit *world*, not *worm*," Quincy reminded him. Max sometimes mixed up his words when he was excited.

"HEY, O DREADED, ANCIENT, GOLDEN PIG-LION-O-DILE —" Max chanted.

Jessica grabbed his shoulder and plopped him into a seat. It was late. Everyone was getting carried away. The meeting hadn't started — and Jessica hadn't told anyone her big news! "Sit down, Max. Look, we can form a special committee to find the eye. We can call Mr. Vorpal. We can go to jewelry shops. We can make a plan. And that's *all* we can do. Okay, now let's have a real meeting!"

No one was listening. Jessica got ready to yell. But she was tired of yelling. She had a better idea.

She made a fist with her left hand. Then she tucked Quincy's cloth napkin into the hole made by her thumb and curved fingers. With her other hand, she began jabbing Max's wand into the napkin — hard.

One by one, the other club members looked at her. Finally, the wand went right through the napkin, right through the hole in Jessica's fist!

"Hey!" Quincy yelled. "My mom just bought me that napkin! She will kill me if it's ripped!"

"Oops — sorry!" Jessica said. She quickly pulled out the wand, and the napkin fell to the table. There was no hole at all.

Everyone stood staring. "Well," Jessica said calmly, "now that I have your attention — this meeting will come to order!"

"Hey, no fair!" Max said. "Tell us how you did that!"

"A magician never reveals her tricks," Jessica replied. "I have some great news. We have a job offer — for our first show ever, outside of school!"

"Like, a real show — for a real audience?" Max asked.

"We'll be superstars," Selena said. "Do we get paid?"

"It's at the Restful Days Elder Care Home," Jessica said. "My great-grandmother lives there. Her name is Gigi, and she loves magic. The show is next Saturday. We can

12

have a rehearsal at my house after dinner tomorrow — *if* Mr. Beamish will give us permission to do this."

Everyone looked at Mr. Beamish. "Please?" Selena asked.

"This is an excellent opportunity," said Quincy.

"I can work on my secret youth potion," Max added. "For our last trick, we'll turn all the old folks into teenagers!"

"Max, if you even *try* that, I'll spill the youth potion on your head," Selena said, "and you'll turn into a teeny little baby!"

Mr. Beamish smiled. "Well, I think this job is a splendid idea."

"All in favor of our first job, say 'Aye'!" Jessica cried out.

"AYE!" shouted Selena and Quincy.

"Goo-goo," said Max.

2

The Jewel in the Quilt

"You would like to do a project on *what*?" asked Mrs. Wegman, the Rebus Elementary School librarian. She gave Quincy a funny smile, as if he had asked a question in Swedish.

"On this ancient, golden pig-lion-o-dile." Quincy put the statue on the library desk. He had spent lunch period cleaning it. Now it was bright and shiny. "We discovered it yesterday. We would like to base our Fourth-Grade Group Research Project on the effect of migration on the history of New England as reflected in the arts and culture of its first settlers. Most specifically, the Vorpal family."

Every year, the fourth-graders had a big research project in social studies. Quincy was sure the statue would make a good topic.

"Did you understand what he said?" Selena whispered to Max and Jessica.

"Just *nod*," hissed Jessica.

Their heads bobbed up and down. "We agree," said Max.

"It looks . . . alive," said Mrs. Wegman, slowly turning pale. "Ms. Tweed? Mr. Hilfer? Will you look at this?"

The two library helpers were trying to hang a big quilt on the wall. But mostly they were arguing. They always argued. Ms. Tweed was thin and pale. She had jet-black hair, with a streak of silver down the middle. Mr. Hilfer was bearded and short and wore dark, thick glasses.

Together, they walked toward the statue. "Ah, a centaur," said Ms. Tweed.

"A centaur is half horse," Mr. Hilfer replied. "This is a satyr."

"A satyr is half goat." Ms. Tweed took the statue and examined it. "Hmm. This is something I've never seen before!"

"Then it needs a proper name," said Mr. Hilfer. "I collect statues of magical beasts, you know, and I name them all after me — Hilferus, Hilfman, Hilfster . . ."

Quincy quickly grabbed the statue back. "He already has a name! It's . . . Grok!"

"*Grok?*" Max whispered. "That *can't* be his name."

"Maybe it has a name tag inside," said Quincy with a shrug. "Let's find the other eye. Then we can open the latch, take out the magic treasure, and see."

"*HEEE-hee-hee-hee-hee!*" came a noise from behind them. It sounded to Jessica like a tree full of sick birds.

Sick, *spying* birds.

Erica Landers and her snobby friends were sitting at a reading table, all crowded on one side. Each girl was holding open a huge history book, but they were all staring at Quincy, Max, and Grok.

"At least *our* group isn't doing a report on a broken-down statue," said Erica, chewing a big pink wad of Big Bubba Bubble Gum.

Jessica reached over and pulled a fashion magazine from Erica's open book. "At least our group is *doing* a report."

17

The girls all quickly shut their books.

Ms. Tweed was already walking toward the back of the library. "Come with me to the stacks," she said with a sigh. "I'll help you find the books you need to do your report."

Quincy, Max, and Selena hurried after her. "The stacks" was a huge room with nothing but bookshelves. It was stuffy and dark and smelly. Jessica didn't like going there at all.

She paused to admire the quilt that hung on the library wall. It had hundreds of different patches sewn together with golden thread. A thick border, sewn with fake diamonds and jewels, ran around the edges.

One of the jewels was very large. And very red.

It was half hidden in the folds, beyond Jessica's reach. She walked closer, grabbed the quilt, pulled — and the jewel peeked through.

It was exactly the same size, shape, and color as the one in Grok's eye.

"QUINCY!" she shouted.

"SSSSSSH!" said Mrs. Wegman.

"*HEEE-hee-hee-hee-hee!*" Erica's friends giggled.

Jessica ran into the stacks. Quincy was sitting all alone in the first row, with a pile of books.

"*Quincy, where's Ms. Tweed?*" Jessica whispered.

"Helping Selena and Max," Quincy said, his nose in a book.

Jessica took him by the shoulders. "I saw it — the other jewel — Grok's missing eye. *It's right here in the library!* Someone sewed it into the quilt on the wall!"

Quincy looked up. "That's crazy."

"Go! Go and look!" Jessica said.

Quincy closed his book, stood up, and tiptoed out of the stacks. He came back very quickly. "I saw it, but I didn't get a good look. Erica was watching me. She's been spying on us since we got here. I was afraid she might suspect."

"Suspect *what*?" Jessica asked.

"Jessica, I think we have something big," Quincy whispered. "Very big. Not only one of the great missing treasures of the world . . . maybe even a link to a lost land!"

Ms. Tweed peeked around the bookcase. "What on Earth are you two talking about?"

"A lost . . . *lamp*!" Quincy said quickly. "In the reading room."

"Really?" said Ms. Tweed, turning away. "Oh, dear, I'll have to go look."

Jessica and Quincy waited until she left. Then they ran around the bookcase and found Max and Selena. Jessica quickly explained about the jewel.

One at a time, Max and Selena sneaked out to look. They raced back, amazed.

"How in the world did it get there?" Selena asked.

"Magic spirits work in strange ways," Max said.

Jessica paced back and forth. "We have to get that jewel."

"That would be stealing!" Quincy scolded. "First, we have to *prove* that the jewel came from Grok. Then we can ask Mrs. Wegman for it. Maybe she will give it to us."

"AND *ABRACADABRA* — ONCE THE EYE IS RETURNED, GROK'S MAGIC POWERS WILL BE RESTORED," Max shouted, waving his wand. "AND WE CLAIM OUR TREASURE!"

"Shhh!" Jessica said. "The whole school will hear us!"

From the reading room, Mrs. Wegman's voice called out, "Time to go back to class, kids. Please check out your books!"

Jessica, Quincy, Max, and Selena scooped up their books. As they ran out to the reading room, Jessica's mind raced. How could they possibly prove that the jewel came from the strange statue? And who — or what — *was* this thing called Grok?

She was the first person in the checkout line. Quincy was behind her. "Don't look at the jewel," he whispered in her ear. "Act normal. Casual."

Max tried to whistle. But he didn't know how, so he just blew.

Jessica looked away. She could see Erica and her friends leaving the library.

"Step up, please, Jessica," Mrs. Wegman said.

As Jessica lifted her books to the table, she caught a last glimpse of the quilt. At the top, there was a tangle of loose threads.

The jewel was gone.

Suspect Number One

"Who could have taken it?" Selena said, rushing down the hallway.

"An evil gremlin, I bet," replied Max. "Or a library leprechaun."

"Preposterous," snapped Quincy.

Max shook his head. "There's no such thing as a preposterous. They're extinct."

"It's not a dinosaur name," Quincy explained. "It means *ridiculous*."

"All I know is, the jewel's gone," said Jessica. "We have to tell Mr. Beamish, and we have to call an emergency meeting of the Abracadabra Club."

"Mystery is our middle name!" cried Quincy.

Down the hall, Erica was standing with her friends just outside Room 104, Mr. Beamish's door. When they saw Quincy and Jessica, they giggled and went into the classroom.

Jessica grabbed Quincy by the arm. "Erica heard us talking about Grok. So she knew about the jewel. She's the thief!"

"She couldn't reach that high," Selena reminded her. "She's too short."

"Good point," Max said, turning toward his classroom, Room 110. "Remember, we can't just blame everybody. We have to really think. We have to make sense. We have to find *proof*!"

Quincy took out his Clues Book. He read aloud as he wrote: " 'Erica Landers . . . possible suspect number one . . .' "

Suddenly, Max spun around. "I know! I know who did it!"

"Who?" asked Jessica, Quincy, and Selena.

Max smiled proudly. "A *flying* leprechaun!"

As soon as school ended, they all raced to the Abracadabra Club room.

"I call this emergency meeting to order!" Jessica said, pulling up a chair. "First item of business — the stolen jewel."

"Leprechauns are out," Max said sadly. "They can't fly. I looked it up."

"You are so weird," Selena said, slowly brushing her hair.

"Some people think brushing your hair all day is weird," Max said.

Quincy wrote in his notepad. "'Three people watched Erica all day. All agreed she was acting strange. . . .'"

The door opened and Mr. Beamish came in, shaking his head. "Sorry I'm late. I was talking to Erica. She says you've been staring at her all day."

Jessica quickly explained about the jewel in the quilt. As Mr. Beamish listened, he began pacing across the front of the room. "This doesn't make sense. Erica wouldn't do something like that. None of my students would."

"No one in this whole school would take someone else's stuff in plain sight," Quincy said.

"Hmm . . . What interesting things you

have in here," said Max, opening Selena's backpack.

"*Ma-a-a-ax!*" Selena shouted, reaching across the table.

Max pulled away. He quickly dug his right hand into the backpack — and pulled out a yellow rubber duck. "Cute. Very cute."

Selena gasped. "That's not mine!"

Max took out a screwdriver. A plastic spider. A football key chain. A dirty rag. A rubber hand. "What, no more hairbrushes?"

Jessica burst out laughing. She knew a magic trick when she saw one.

"Thank you! Thank you!" Max said, taking a bow.

"Very funny," Selena said. "Now give it back."

Mr. Beamish tried to look angry. "Max, that was well done. But you should have asked for Selena's permission first."

Max began to close up the bag. Then his smile quickly disappeared. He gave Selena a long, serious look, then reached into her bag one last time.

He pulled out a large ruby-red jewel.

4
Keeping an Eye Out

"It's not mine!" Selena cried. "I — I never saw it before!"

Jessica thought back to the library. Selena was the only one of the Abracadabra Club who *could* have taken it. "You went out to see the jewel in the quilt, after Quincy and Max," said Jessica. "You were alone. You took it without any of us seeing."

"You must have used a ladder," Quincy said.

"Ladder?" Selena said. "Have you lost your mind?"

Max suddenly burst out laughing, as if he had just pulled a great joke.

"Wait — *you* put the jewel in there, Max?" Mr. Beamish asked.

Max nodded, laughing so hard he had to sit down. "I fooled you all!"

"So . . . *you're* the thief, Max?" Jessica asked. "You stole the jewel?"

Max froze. "No! I mean, yes! I mean, I did put the jewel in Selena's bag. But it's not real. I found it in my house, in my old toy box. It was just part of the trick, that's all."

Selena was furious. "Here's a *really* good trick — I will make a fourth-grader disappear," she said, lifting her hairbrush. "Oh, Maxie? Come, let me fix your hair . . ."

Max ran screaming from the room.

Jessica could hardly sleep that night. It was all because of Grok. She put him on her desk, but his eyes glowed in the light of her Bugs Bunny night-light. She put him on her dresser, but his eyes glowed in the streetlight from outside. She thought of throwing him out the window. But she couldn't do that. She had to be with Grok, all the time. Whoever stole the jewel might try to steal him, too. So Grok spent the night under her pillow.

All the next day, he stayed in her backpack. By lunchtime, he was getting too heavy, so she put Grok on the table in the cafeteria.

Four seats away, Andrew Flingus grinned. His teeth were covered with bits of sardine sandwich, Cracker Jack crumbs, and pieces of chocolate doughnut holes. Jessica suddenly felt sick.

Which was the usual feeling she had around Andrew Flingus. Some people said he was the most awful boy in the fourth grade. Some said he was the most awful child in the history of the world. The truth was somewhere in between.

"Hey, Greek," Andrew said, aiming a doughnut hole at the statue. "Open wide! HAR! HAR! HAR!"

"His name is *Grok*," said Jessica, pulling the statue away.

The doughnut hole flew high — right toward Quincy.

Quincy grabbed it in midair. He looked at it oddly. "Andrew, what did you do to this? It feels like rubber."

He threw the doughnut hole down to the

floor. It bounced back up, high over the table, like a rubber ball!

Andrew was so surprised, he nearly choked on his sandwich. He began spitting out bits of sardines and Cracker Jack. Other kids ran for cover.

Smiling, Quincy threw the doughnut hole down again. Up it bounced again. Now everyone in the cafeteria was laughing. Except for Mr. Snodgrass, the cafeteria teacher. He had only smiled once that year, the day they served spinach bean soup.

Andrew was looking closely at Grok now. He climbed on the table. He tried to sit the way Grok was sitting. He stuck out his mouth like Grok's snout. "HAR! HAR! HAR!" he said. "Look at me — I'm Gork!"

He pulled a large red jewel out of his shirt pocket, then put it over his right eye.

"Holy Houdini!" Max cried out. "Andrew has the jewel!"

Jessica nearly dived across the table. "Give that to us!"

"Huh?" Andrew fell to the floor. He landed with a squish.

The jewel rolled away, into the kitchen.

"*Get it!*" shouted Max. He, Jessica, Quincy, and Selena jumped over Andrew. They raced into the kitchen. They saw the jewel bounce off the wall.

With a *clickety-click*, it disappeared down a metal drain in the floor.

"NO-O-O!" shouted Jessica. She grabbed the drain and tried to pull it up.

"You won't get it, dearie," said Mrs. Barstow, the lunch lady. "There's a pipe under there. It goes straight to the duck pond."

"The duck pond?" Max pushed his magic wand forward like a sword. "CHA-A-ARGE!"

He ran back through the cafeteria, his cape flying. Jessica, Selena, and Quincy followed close behind. Everyone was screaming and laughing, except Mr. Snodgrass. He just looked sour.

The Abracadabra Club raced out the back of the school, across the parking lot, and through the gate to the duck pond.

The Rebus Duck Pond was shaped like a lima bean, only much bigger, with a cement path around it. A little girl and her dad stood at the edge. They were throwing small pieces of bread into the water.

"Where's the drainpipe?" Quincy asked.

"How should I know?" Max replied.

They walked closer. A fat white duck was poking its beak over the ledge. It bit down hard — but not on a piece of bread.

In its beak was something shiny. And red.

"GET THAT DUCK!" Jessica shouted.

5

Woobies, Worms, and Wrappers

"I, MAX THE MAGNIFICENT, WILL SAVE THE DAY!" Max cried out, running toward the duck pond.

"You can swim?" Quincy asked.

Max stopped short. "No."

"We can't go in there!" Selena said. "The water is all yucky."

The water was brownish-gray and full of

feathers. Jessica thought about wading in, but she couldn't see the bottom.

The duck was swimming away fast. And the little girl was crying so loud, it was hard to think.

"WAAAHHHH! MY WOOBY! MINE!" the girl screamed.

Her dad picked her up and hugged her. "It's okay, sweetie. We'll get you another one."

The girl threw a box of Cracker Jack on the ground. "NO! I WANT *THAT* WOOBY!"

Jessica looked at Quincy. "Wooby?" she said.

"Oh, no . . ." Quincy slapped himself on the forehead. "*Ruby* — that was her ruby! Her Cracker Jack toy. We're on a wild-goose chase."

"Goose?" Max scratched his head. "I thought it was a duck."

"Wait — *Andrew* was eating Cracker Jack," Selena said. "*His* jewel must have come out of the box, too."

"Now we're right back where we started," Quincy said, writing quickly in his notepad. "'Left school building on false alarm . . . Possible big trouble with Mr. Snodgrass . . .'"

They ran into the cafeteria just as the bell rang.

Mr. Snodgrass was busy yelling at Andrew Flingus. He didn't even notice Jessica, Quincy, Max, and Selena.

Four kids running to the duck pond was not as bad as one kid putting sardines up his nose.

After school, Jessica walked home with Quincy and her six-year-old brother, Noah. In a few hours, the whole Abracadabra Club

43

would be coming over to her house to practice for the Restful Days magic show. But she couldn't even think of the practice.

The only thing on her mind was Erica. She had been acting weird all day. Which was why Jessica, Quincy, and Noah had decided to follow her home from school.

Erica was talking with her friend, Charlene Crump. Charlene was about ninety percent hair. It was like a big salad of curls, spilling over her face, covering her eyes.

Jessica and Quincy tried to stay silent. Noah did, too, for about one minute.

"Ooh! I know who took the jewel — a worm!" Noah blurted out. "Andrew Flingus told me the liberry is full of bookworms."

"SSHHH!" said Jessica. "Erica will hear us!"

"We're too far behind her," Quincy whispered. "She can't hear a thing."

Erica turned around and made a face. "That's what you think."

Jessica pulled Quincy and Noah across the street. "Noah, you have a big mouth."

"And you have a Carrot-head," Noah replied. He knew Jessica hated that nickname.

"Jessica, I've got it," Quincy said, scribbling in his notepad. "We're doing this backward. We shouldn't be going after the thief. We'll let the thief come to us."

"That's crazy," Jessica whispered. "We need that jewel *now*, Quincy —"

"Yes, but the thief needs Grok, too," Quincy said. "So if we just hold onto Grok long enough, the crook will *have* to come to us. If the crook is Erica, we will demand the jewel — and if she says no, we'll turn her in to Mr. McElroy."

"Great, Quincy, great. And what if the

crook isn't Erica — what if it's Mr. Hilfer or Ms. Tweed? Or a real thief! Then what do we do?"

Quincy began writing again. "I'm working on it."

At the corner of Dunster Street, Jessica and Noah said good-bye to Quincy and turned left. They could smell their dad's cooking a block away. Their mom hardly ever made dinner, which was kind of funny, because she was a *real* cook. She owned a food shop called Into the Kitchen, but she always came home late.

"Hey, Noah, comin' through the doah . . ." Mr. Frimmel sang to the tune on the kitchen radio. "Wipe your shoes, Jessie, don't be messy!"

"Smells great!" Jessica said. She kissed her dad and ran upstairs to do homework.

She had until 5:30. Then she would have

to help with dinner — and after dinner was the magic show practice.

Jessica went right to work. But she was halfway through math when she heard a scraping noise.

It came from the side of the house. From the bushes near the dining room. At first she thought it was her mom. But Mrs. Frimmel's car wasn't in the driveway.

Jessica ran downstairs. She scooted through the kitchen and tiptoed into the dining room.

CRASH!

The noise made her jump. Outside the window, the bushes rustled sharply. Jessica heard a muffled "Yeeps!"

She ran outside. Quincy was standing just outside the dining room.

"What are you doing, sneaking around like that?" Jessica demanded.

"Correction," Quincy said. "I was merely walking up your front lawn. A bit early for the magic show practice, but I like to be early. I spied a gum wrapper. It was Big Bubba Bubble Gum, and I know you do not chew that brand. So I decided to investigate. And that was when I saw the intruder!"

Jessica knew only one person who chewed Big Bubba Bubble Gum. "Erica?"

"Our number-one suspect," Quincy said. "Caught red-handed."

6

Grok Shock

In Room 104, everyone was packing up books and papers. The class was going to the library with Mr. Hilfer to work on their group reports.

"Bushes? Hiding? Me?" Erica said to Jessica. "Why would I want to go to your cootie house? I was with Charlene yesterday. We were working on our group report."

"But Quincy saw you on my front lawn!" Jessica said.

"How did he know it was Erica?" asked Charlene Crump, pushing aside her wild brown curls. "Maybe it was someone who *looked* like her."

"Come, come — hurry, hurry," said Mr. Hilfer, who was waiting by the door.

Slowly, a stack of papers and books rose from Quincy's desk. His arms were underneath, lifting them. But his face could not be seen.

With a sudden crash, everything tumbled to the floor — including Quincy.

Jessica groaned. Erica and Charlene giggled like crazy.

"Come on, we'll be late," Selena said to Jessica.

They hurried down the hall to the library. Inside, Ms. Tweed was dusting a stack of old books on a table.

It reminded Jessica of a magic trick.

"Watch this," she whispered to Selena.

Jessica went to Ms. Tweed's table, opened one of the old, dusty books and leafed through it. "Wow, these books must be really valuable. Feel this paper. So old, but so strong."

"These are from my family collection," Ms. Tweed said with a smile. "They're mostly from my mother's house. Books she read to me as a child. I'm donating them to the library."

"Yes, very strong paper . . ." Jessica grabbed a fashion magazine out of Selena's hands. She ripped the corners off the two center pages and handed them to Ms. Tweed. "Compare it to this cheap paper."

"Hey, I was reading that!" said Selena.

Ms. Tweed took the scraps. "Jessica, there was no need to damage the magazine."

Jessica rested her hand on the pile of old books. "Wow, that paper is *so* good, I can feel the words of the books entering my brain. Quick, Ms. Tweed, I'll prove it to you. Just add up the page numbers of those scraps I gave you. Don't tell me the answer! Just add them up."

Ms. Tweed looked confused. "Why . . . all right. There. I've done it. But —"

Jessica spread out three of Ms. Tweed's old books. "Now, pick two of these."

Ms. Tweed pointed to *Treasure Island* and *If I Ran the Zoo*.

"Now, out of *those* two, pick one," Jessica said.

This time Ms. Tweed pointed to *Treasure Island*.

Jessica handed the book to her. "Now, turn to the page that's the same number as the one you added up. And I'll tell you the first word on that page."

"All right . . ." said Ms. Tweed, opening the book to a page. "Go ahead."

"Um . . . uh . . . let me think . . ." Jessica said. "The word is . . . raisins."

"*Raisins*?" said Selena.

Ms. Tweed's jaw dropped open. "Yes! How on Earth did you do that?"

She was answered by a "Yeeps!" and a *splat* from the front of the library.

Quincy had finally arrived. So had Max's class. Quincy and his papers were all over the floor.

Max, Jessica, and Selena raced over to help. They scooped up everything and put it all on a reading table. Out in the hallway, Jessica could see Erica and Charlene walking toward the library. "Quick," Jessica said, "hide Grok."

"Grok?" Quincy said, looking around. "I — I must have left him in class. I had so much to carry —"

"Quincy, Grok's too valuable to leave in class!" Jessica said. She raced into the hallway. She nearly knocked over Erica. She almost collided with Mr. Hilfer.

When she got to Room 104, Mr. Beamish looked up from his desk. "Forget something?" he asked her.

Jessica went straight to Quincy's desk. Max, Selena, and Quincy were right behind her, checking the floor and tabletops.

But they were too late. Grok was gone.

7

Burglar Among the Books?

Be calm, Jessica said to herself. *Think clearly. Do not raise your voice.*

"YOU PROMISED TO NEVER LET GROK OUT OF YOUR SIGHT, QUINCY!" she screamed.

"I got nervous," Quincy said. "No one was helping me carry all my books. You all had left. Mr. Hilfer was telling me to hurry. Erica and Charlene were laughing at me!"

Erica and Charlene — of course! Jessica thought. That was why they were the last ones out of the room. That was why they were giggling. They *wanted* to make Quincy nervous, so he would forget the statue and they could take it!

"Mr. Beamish?" Jessica asked. "After Selena and I left, did you see anyone picking up the statue?"

"Oh, dear," Mr. Beamish replied. "I was busy grading papers."

Jessica nodded. "Then I call an Abracadabra Club meeting in the hallway, right now!"

As they rushed outside, Quincy opened a notepad. "We now face two mysteries — the stolen jewel and the stolen statue," he said. "This could have been done by two different people. Or it could be the work of one diabolical mind."

"I vote for the dibble — the buy-a-dollic — the one mind!" Max said.

"Maybe Erica wasn't tall enough to steal the jewel in the quilt," Selena said, "but she sure could have taken Grok!"

"Wait a minute . . ." Quincy said, reading something in his notepad. "Erica was not the only one in the room just now. Mr. Hilfer was, too."

"He's a librarian," Max said. "Librarians don't steal. Do they?"

"He has a motive," Quincy said. "He collects statues of mythological creatures. Grok is a creature no one has ever seen before. Very valuable. And worth much more with *two* eyes than with one! And, of course, Mr. Hilfer could reach the jewel."

"Yyyyyesss!" cried Max. "You're a genius, Quincy! Case solved!"

"Except for one important thing," Selena said. "How do we get Grok back?"

"I'm working on that," said Quincy. "For now, we must go back to the library, act normal, and watch our suspect." He scooted down the hall, with Selena and Max close behind.

Jessica followed slowly. Something wasn't right. Mr. Hilfer didn't seem like the kind of person who would steal. Besides, he loved to show off his magical figures in school. Some of them seemed valuable, too. He couldn't bring a stolen statue to school. Everyone would know where Grok had come from.

What was the point of stealing a statue you had to hide?

In the library, Jessica tried to work, but it was impossible. She couldn't stop staring at Mr. Hilfer.

He was near the quilt wall, behind Mrs.

Wegman and Ms. Tweed. He had cleared off part of an old bookshelf and was dusting it.

As he turned away, something fell to the floor with a thud.

"Oh, dear, Mr. Hilfer!" Ms. Tweed cried out. "Must you leave your things on the floor?"

She knelt down and picked something up.

"Ms. Tweed — no!" Mr. Hilfer cried out.

Ms. Tweed stood. She held out an object wrapped in a paper bag.

It was exactly the size of Grok.

8

Senior Moment

"Ladies and gents!" said a gray-haired man named Mr. Finney. "Let's welcome the Abracadabra Club to the Restful Days Elder Care Home!"

"Hip-hip-hooray!" came a shout from the back of the crowd.

"That's my great-granddaughter!" said Gigi proudly, pointing at Jessica. Gigi was very stiff from something called Arthur Itis, but she was always full of life. She smiled all the time, and her soft voice reminded Jessica of a tinkling music box.

The rec room at the elder care home was packed. A big sign that said WELCOME ABRACADABRA CLUB had been strung against the back wall. Chairs, sofas, and wheelchairs faced a small stage at one end. Gigi sat in front. She led all the cheering. Most people in the group were smiling and clapping. But a woman with a sad face sat quietly next to Gigi, fanning herself with a napkin. She looked somehow familiar, but Jessica couldn't figure out why.

Up on the stage, the Abracadabra Club took a bow. They were gathered around a rickety table that held all their props. It also held a huge deck of cards that Selena had made from oaktag the night before. As they stood up, Selena took out her hairbrush.

"I'm sooo nervous," she whispered, furiously brushing her hair.

"*Put that thing away!*" Quincy hissed.

Jessica stepped forward. She didn't feel nervous, just confused. Mr. Hilfer was on her mind. How could he have taken Grok? Why?

And how in the world were they going to get the statue and jewel back?

Think, Jessica, think! she told herself.

"Um . . . for our first trick," she said, raising a magic wand, "I shall place this wand in a bottle — and it will rise out of the bottle all by itself!"

"Hip-hip-hooray!" called a voice from the back.

"Please ignore Mr. Buford," said Gigi in a loud whisper. "He says 'hip-hip-hooray' to cvcrything."

Jessica placed a large, dark glass bottle

on the table. She put the magic wand inside, so that the top was sticking out.

The room fell silent. Jessica slowly waved her hand over the wand. But nothing happened.

"Uh-oh, I'll have to try harder," she said.

She rubbed her hands together, then tried again.

The wand twitched. Then, slowly, it began to rise up out of the bottle!

"Bravo!" cried Gigi. "Isn't she wonderful?"

The whole crowd clapped, except for Mr. Buford, who had fallen asleep in the back.

"AND NOW," said Max, whooshing his cape, "I, MAX THE MAGNIFICENT, WILL DO AN AMAZING TRICK TO ASTOUND THE SENSES! BUT FIRST, I NEED A VOLUNTEER TO GIVE ME A NURSE!"

"*Purse,*" Quincy whispered.

"I MEAN, PURSE!" Max said.

Gigi happily handed him her purse.

"Madam, what strange things you carry!" Max said. He pulled out a plastic duck, a fake spider, a tube of sparkles, a toy truck — and a rubber hand.

"Hip-hip —" shouted Mr. Buford, and then he fell asleep again.

Jessica had never seen Gigi giggle so hard. The woman next to her was smiling, just a little bit.

And when Quincy asked for a volunteer for the next trick, Gigi tapped that woman with her elbow. "Go ahead, Betty, you like magic."

The woman slowly rolled herself forward in her wheelchair. "You won't fool me, young man!"

Quincy held out a quarter. "Hold out

your palm — and on the count of three, grab this quarter and don't let go." Quincy counted, "One . . . two . . ." very slowly, each time pressing the quarter into her palm, then lifting it back up again.

When he brought his hand down and said ". . . three!" Betty closed her hand tight. But when she opened it, it was empty!

Quincy pretended to be shocked. He leaned slowly forward — and the quarter fell out of the sky, into Betty's hand.

"Oh!" Betty cried out. "Oh, dear! That is marvelous!"

The rest of the show passed by in a happy blur. By the end, even Mr. Buford had awakened. And when the show ended, he "hip-hip-hooray"-ed as loud as ever.

At the curtain call, Jessica forgot to bow. She was too busy watching all the people. All the old faces seemed so young when they were smiling.

That was the most magical thing of all.

Jessica ran off the stage to Gigi, who kissed her about a hundred times. Her parents kissed her. Gigi kissed Noah. Jessica tried to kiss Noah, too, but he ran away, screaming.

Betty had vanished, but now she came wheeling back into the rec room. In her lap, she held a rolled-up blanket. "Jessica, darling, your group made me feel like a young girl again," she said. "And I would like to give you all a gift. It's something I've just finished."

As she unrolled the fabric, the Abracadabra Club gathered around. And Jessica saw that it wasn't a blanket at all. It was a quilt. A quilt made of gorgeous patches of material, sewn together with fine gold thread.

Jessica's mouth nearly dropped open. "It's . . . so cool! It looks just like —"

"The one at the school library!" Quincy exclaimed.

Betty gave a faraway smile. "I made another quilt like this once. I worked on it for months, many years ago. I made it for my daughter, Lucy. She wanted to give it to a young man, the love of her life. He was a magician, too."

"Betty, was there a red jewel in the quilt?" Jessica asked.

Betty's smile faded. "No, dear. But Lucy and her boyfriend added things to the quilt as their love grew. Sadly, the romance didn't last. He went to Vermont. My daughter donated the quilt to the school library, so she could see it every day . . ."

Jessica's heart nearly skipped a beat. Now she knew why Betty looked familiar.

"Did your daughter also donate books to the school library?" Jessica asked. "Old books from your house?"

"Why, yes, of course," Betty said.

"Betty," Jessica said, "is your daughter Ms. Tweed?"

9

Vorpal Strikes Again

"Hello?" Jessica said, peeking into the library. It was 7:45, fifteen minutes before school started. Jessica, Quincy, Selena, and Max had come to school extra early to try to solve the mystery.

The library was strangely quiet, as if it had been covered by a thick curtain. The air had the musty, sweet smell of old books.

Ms. Tweed was all alone, tidying up.

"Well, well," she said. "Fourth-graders in the library at this hour? What a treat. Come in."

"We came to see you, Ms. Tweed," Jessica said softly. "We met your mom yesterday. She's really nice. She's friends with my great-grandmother, at the nursing home."

"How lovely," Ms. Tweed said. "I hope she was nice to you. She can be . . . quiet."

"She told us all about herself, and about you, too," Jessica went on. "And she also mentioned the quilt on the library wall. She said it was very special to you."

"There was a red jewel in the quilt," Quincy said. "We noticed it because it looked just like the other eye of our statue. But it just disappeared one day . . ."

Ms. Tweed's eyes became distant. She took a deep breath, and when she spoke her voice was soft and faraway. "That jewel was given to me by a wonderful man. I could never bear to see it go. In the stacks that afternoon, I heard you talking about it. About how it matched the eye of the statue. And I was afraid . . ."

"But we would never steal it!" Selena said.

Ms. Tweed smiled. "Of course you wouldn't. You would ask Mrs. Wegman for it. And I was afraid she would give it to you. You see, it's not a real ruby. It's not really worth anything — except to me. So I took it, for safekeeping. It's the only reminder I have of Victor."

"*Victor*?" Jessica squeaked. She knew a Victor who was a magician. He lived in Vermont, too — and he was probably Ms. Tweed's age.

"Do you mean Victor Vorpal?" Max asked. "The guy who owns Frost Village, where we went on a fourth-grade long weekend? With the white beard, who makes birds

72

fly out of his sleeve? Who gave us the treasure chest that had Grok in it? *That* Victor Vorpal?"

"Yes," said Ms. Tweed with a sigh. "That marvelous, magical fellow . . ."

Jessica had to sit down. Their adventure in Frost Village seemed so far away. The deep woods, the lodge, the mysterious maps, the hidden chest with magic treasure.

Ms. Tweed walked behind the front desk. She reached into a drawer and pulled out the red jewel. "Here," she said. "It's not good to hold onto memories."

"Are you sure?" Selena asked.

"Sure," said Ms. Tweed.

Quincy put a big ✔ on the "Missing Jewel" page of the Abracadabra Club Mystery Log. "Now if we only had Grok, we could find what treasures are hidden inside," he said.

"You haven't seen the statue, have you?" Selena asked Ms. Tweed. "Like, in that bag that Mr. Hilfer told you not to touch?"

"This?" Reaching back to the shelf, Ms. Tweed pulled out the paper bag. She took a huge Thermos out of it. "Mrs. Wegman does not allow us to eat or drink in here. But dear old Mr. Hilfer does love his coffee, and sometimes he hides it."

Jessica groaned. If that was coffee, then Mr. Hilfer was innocent. Which meant the statue could only have been taken by . . .

Whack!

The library door swung open hard. Erica and Charlene burst into the library. "*She* took it!" Erica said, pointing to Jessica. "Jessica Frimmel is a thief!"

10

The Secret Revealed

"Jessica Frimmel stole the jewel from the rug on the wall!" Erica announced. "She wanted it for her statue. I heard her talk about it. And Quincy's in on it, too."

"Call the police!" Charlene said.

Jessica looked at Ms. Tweed. "Uh, thank you, girls," said Ms. Tweed, holding up the jewel. "But we have it already."

"Good!" Erica replied. "And we have *this*!"

She reached into her backpack and proudly pulled out — Grok!

Jessica couldn't believe it. He was all covered with chewed gum and chocolate stains. "*You* had him all this time — and you did *that* to him?"

"Don't worry, he's been safe with us," Charlene said proudly, placing Grok on the desk. "We took him so you wouldn't get him."

Ms. Tweed handed Jessica the jewel. Jessica held it between her thumb and two fingers. Carefully, she put it in the eye socket.

As it snapped into place, both rubies caught the reflection of the ceiling light. They flashed brightly.

With a soft *click,* a small door opened

in the back of the statue. And something dropped out.

It was a silver locket, oval-shaped and worn.

"Ahem," Erica said, clearing her throat. "I think I deserve some sort of reward?"

Charlene nudged her in the ribs. "We split it half and half."

Ms. Tweed dug her fingernails into the locket and pried it open. The rusty hinge snapped. The two halves of the locket fell faceup on the desk. Each side held a photo covered with yellowed, broken glass. One was of a young man with dark hair and eyes like fire. The other was of a young woman with long hair and a strong, sunny face.

Engraved in each silver frame were the words VICTOR AND LUCY FOREVER.

Victor Vorpal and Lucy Tweed, Jessica said to herself. They looked so young.

Ms. Tweed was smiling, but her eyes were wet.

"That's the dumbest, oldest, yuckiest reward I ever saw," said Erica. She pointed her nose in the air and marched out of the library. "Come, Charlene. What a waste of time!"

"Yeah," said Charlene, following close behind.

Jessica looked at Quincy. Quincy looked at Selena. Selena looked at Max. They all looked at Ms. Tweed.

Then they all laughed so hard, they didn't even hear the school bell ring.

Quincy put a mark in his Mystery Log. "Case closed!"

The Abracadabra Files by Quincy
Magic Trick #11
Wand Through a Napkin

Ingredients:
One magic wand
One cloth napkin

How Jessica did it:

1. She made a fist. The back of her hand was facing us. She spread the napkin over the top of the fist. Then she poked the wand into the napkin, just above the little hole made by her thumb and index finger. That made a little "dent" in the napkin.
2. Under the napkin, she let her thumb and index finger come apart a bit. Now they formed a C-shape. Then she poked the wand again. Part of the napkin (the part we couldn't see) drooped down into her fist. That allowed the wand to slide down along the opening.

3. Once the napkin (and the wand) was
   through, she tightened her grip again.
   When she pushed the wand all the way
   down, it looked as if it had made a hole!

How the wand goes
through the napkin from
the audience's point of
view.

How the wand goes through
the napkin from your
point of view.

The Abracadabra Files by Quincy
Magic Trick #12
How'd THAT Get in My Pack?

Ingredients:
A friend's backpack
Hollow rubber hand
Rubber duck, screwdriver, plastic spider,
football key chain, dirty rag (or ANYTHING
weird — this trick will work with any items
that fit inside a rubber hand)

How Max Did It:

1. At home, he had stuffed the silly stuff
    into the rubber hand. He kept the hand in
    his backpack during school. Then, just
    before the meeting, he put it in his back
    pocket. (It was sticking out a little bit,
    but we couldn't see it because of his
    cape.)
2. When he opened Selena's backpack and
    said, "What interesting things you
    have," we all looked, too. While we
    were looking, he grabbed the rubber
    hand from his back pocket.

82

3.   He reached into the backpack with the
     rubber hand. But we didn't notice —
     because all our attention was on the
     pack! Then he pulled the funny things
     out of the hand inside the backpack.

The Abracadabra Files by Quincy
Magic Trick #13
The Floating Wand in the Bottle

Ingredients:
One magic wand
One long bottle, wide enough to put the
wand in but shorter than the wand
Very thin string or thread

How Jessica Did It:

1. Before the trick started, she attached
    one end of the thread to the edge of
    the table, the other end to the wand.
2. She put the wand into the bottle, string-
    end first.
3. With her left hand, she grabbed the bot-
    tle near the bottom. As she waved her
    right hand "magically" over the wand,
    she slowly slid the bottle away from
    her. That made the string pull on the
    wand — and lift it out of the bottle!

The Abracadabra Files by Quincy
Magic Trick #14
It's Raining Quarters!

Ingredients:
One quarter

How I Did It:

I pressed the quarter into Betty's hand slowly. "One . . ." Then I lifted the quarter way over my head, and slowly pressed it against her palm again. "Two . . ." I lifted it way over my head again. But this time, *I kept it there*! I actually put the quarter on my head. When I brought my hand down and said, "Three!" there was nothing in it. Betty closed her hand into a fist — and when she opened it, nothing was there. But because I had pressed it into her hand, it felt like the quarter was still there!

All I had to do was tilt my head forward. The quarter fell — and it seemed to be coming out of the sky.

About the Author

Peter Lerangis is the author of many different kinds of books for many ages, including *Watchers*, an award-winning science-fiction/mystery series; *Antarctica*, a two-book exploration adventure; and several hilarious novels for young readers, including *Spring Fever!*, *Spring Break*, *It Came from the Cafeteria*, and *Attack of the Killer Potatoes*. His recent movie adaptations include *The Sixth Sense* and *El Dorado*. He lives in New York City with his wife, Tina deVaron, and their two sons, Nick and Joe.